Bonkers For Conkers
A World Book Day Poetry Book

Bonkers For Conkers

A World Book Day Poetry Book

Chosen by
Gaby Morgan

Illustrated by
Jane Eccles

MACMILLAN CHILDREN'S BOOKS

*For Evie – who is brand new – and Grant and Jude
with all my love. A huge thank you to Rachel and
Anna for filling my shoes so brilliantly.*

First published 2003
by Macmillan Children's Books
a division of Macmillan Publishers Limited
20 New Wharf Road, London N1 9RR
Basingstoke and Oxford
www.panmacmillan.com

Associated companies throughout the world

ISBN 0 330 41593 X

3 5 7 9 8 6 4 2

A CIP catalogue record for this book is available from the British Library.

Printed by Mackays of Chatham plc, Chatham, Kent.

Contents

The Prince and the Snail

Once, in a castle
a Prince loved a snail.
He painted the shell gold
and kept the snail in his pocket.

The King and the Queen
thought the Prince mad.
'It must be a difficult relationship,'
said the King.
'Why?' asked the Prince.
(Love makes you that way.)

The Queen said,
'Son, let's talk.
You see, there're certain things
you can do
and certain things
you cannot do
and, I'm afraid,
kissing a snail in public
is most definitely out.'

The Prince said to the snail,
'This is hopeless.
We'll have to run away.'
'Mmmm,' said the snail.
(Again, love makes you that way.)

So the Prince ran away
with the golden snail.
They ran to the edge
of the land
and sat on the beach.

'Phew,' said the Prince.
'I'm out of breath.'
'Take me out of your pocket!'
gasped the snail.
'I'm suffocating!'

Then, in the sea,
a huge black monster appeared.
It looked at the Prince
and winked.
'A whale!' said the snail.
'What a flirt!' said the Prince.

That night the Prince
swam out to the whale.
The whale was as big as a castle.
'I love you!' said the Prince.
'Glug, glug!' said the snail.

'Why not live in my belly?'
gurgled the whale.
(You know how whales are.)
So the Prince crawled inside.
'It's dark,' said the Prince.
'I love you,' said the whale.

Once, in a belly,
a Prince loved a whale.
As if the belly were a pocket
and the Prince a golden snail.

Philip Ridley

House Party

The houses had a party
they invited all their friends –
the semis and the terraced
the middles and the ends.
They invited all the chalets,
high-rise blocks of flats,
caravans and castles,
homes for dogs and cats.

They invited all the bungalows,
houses from Peru,
scrapers from Big Apple,
huts from Timbuktu.
The igloos came,
the teepees,
pagodas and a cave,
an ant hill,
and a beehive,
a police house
and a nave.

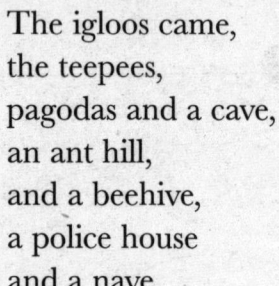

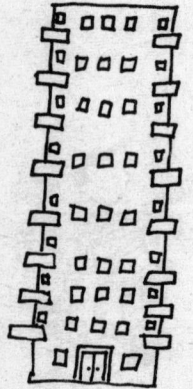

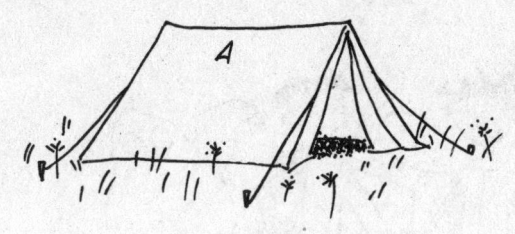

It was a lovely party –
the church house did some chants,
the summer house brought sunshine,
and the greenhouse brought the plants.
 The lighthouse winked a message
 for peace within each house . . .
 'Hallelujah' sang the angels
 'Hallelujah' sighed the mouse.

Peter Dixon

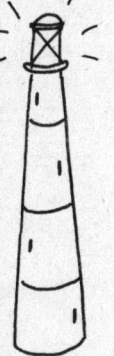

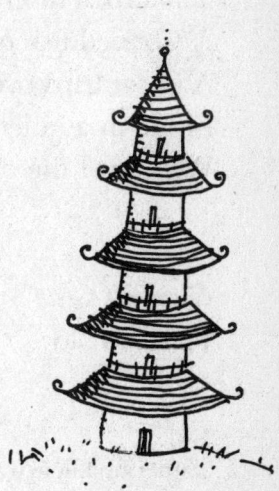

World Book Day Blues

Playtime.
Cinderella munches crisps.
Tinkerbell loses her hairband.
A worried teacher separates a sword-fighting duo.
A ghost trips over his sheet.
I hide in a quiet corner.
Why am I the only one not dressed up?

Catherine Glew
11 years old

Catherine Glew was the winner of the Macmillan Poem
on a Postcard Competition 2002.

Horribly Thin Poem

One winter evening,
When everything
Was dark,
And everyone was
Safely indoors,
I had to walk
Home
Alone,
All alone,
Through
Dark
Cold,
Creepy,
Silent
Streets . . .

And I thought
Hello!
There's
A
Shadow . . .
A
Dark,
Mysterious shadow,
In that
Doorway

Over there . . .
What will I do?
If the door
Opens
Just
As
I walk past,
And
A great
Ugly
HAND
Comes out
And grabs me?
What will I do?
WHAT will I do?
What WILL I do?
What will I DO?
And I ran
And ran
And ran
Right past that door.

And when I was past it,
I stopped
And looked back
And said:
'Ha ha!
You didn't get me that time!'

And a
Cold
Shivery
Croaky
Broken
Old voice
Slithered
Out of the letterbox
And said
'No, but just you wait,
There's always
Another
Time . . .'

David Orme

The Magic of the Brain

Such a sight I saw:
An eight-sided kite surging up into a cloud
Its eight tails streaming out as if they were one.
It lifted my heart as starlight lifts the head
Such a sight I saw.

And such a sound I heard.
One bird through dim winter light as the day was
    closing
Poured out a song suddenly from an empty tree.
It cleared my head as water refreshes the skin
Such a sound I heard.

Such a smell I smelled:
A mixture of roses and coffee, of green leaf and
   warmth.
It took me to gardens and summer and cities abroad,
Memories of meetings as if my past friends were
   here
Such a smell I smelled.

Such soft fur I felt.
It wrapped me around, soothing my winter-cracked
   skin,
Not gritty or stringy or sweaty but silkily warm
As my animal slept on my lap, and we both breathed
   content
Such soft fur I felt.

Such food I tasted:
Smooth-on-tongue soup, and juicy crackling of meat,
Greens like fresh fields, sweet-on-your-palate peas,
Jellies and puddings with fragrance of fruit they are
    made from
Such good food I tasted.

Such a world comes in:
Far world of the sky to breathe in through your nose
Near world you feel underfoot as you walk on the
    land.
Through your eyes and your ears and your mouth
    and your brilliant brain
Such a world comes in.

Jenny Joseph

Sonnet Number One

The moon doth shine as bright as in the day
I sit upon the seesaw wondering why
She left me. Boys and girls come out to play.
But I'm bereft. I think I'm going to cry.
I gave her chocolate and I praised her skill
At skateboarding and football not to mention
Arm wrestling. As we slowly climbed the hill
To fetch some water, did I sense a tension?
She seemed preoccupied. She hardly spoke
And as we turned the handle to the well
I asked her, Jill, please tell me it's a joke.
She said, I've found another bloke. I fell,
I spun, head over heels into the dark
Down to the bottom where I broke my heart.

Roger Stevens

Grandma Was Eaten by a Shark!

Grandma was eaten by a shark
Dad, by a killer whale
And my baby brother got slurped up
By a rather hungry sea snail.

A cuttlefish cut my mum to bits
An octopus strangled my sister
A jellyfish stung my auntie's toes
Giving her terrible blisters.

A pufferfish poisoned my grandpa
A dogfish ate my cat
And then a catfish ate my dog!
I was very upset about that.

So you go for a swim if you like
Just don't ask me to come too
I'm staying here with my camera
I can't wait to see what gets you!

Andrea Shavick

It's Spring Again

It's spring again,
But this year everything's different.
Grandad's vegetable patch isn't dug
And the man who came to mow the lawn
Didn't do it in stripes
Like Grandad did.

When I went with Grandma
To visit Grandad's grave,
The daffodils we planted in the autumn
Were in full bloom.
'He'd have liked them,
Wouldn't he, Grandma?' I said.
'Yes,' she said. 'He would have.'

John Foster

The Mysterious Employment of God

To each and every blade of grass,
Apply a coat of whitest gloss.
Brush the trees (on one side)
Soften hills, far and wide.
Solder horizon, cloud and sky,
Make the join invisible to eye.
Windows, wipe with flakes of frost,
Teach smoke to drift, pretend it's lost.
Dress the hedge with spider thread,
Turn to statues flowerbed.
Icicles hang at edge of stream,
Allow the hidden buds to dream.

Andrew Fusek Peters

The Giantess

Where can I find seven small girls to be pets,
where can I find them?
One to comb the long grass of my hair
with this golden rake,
one to dig with this copper spade
the dirt from under my nails.
I will pay them in crab-apples.

Where can I find seven small girls to help me,
where can I find them?
A third to scrub at my tombstone teeth
with this mop in its bronze bucket,
a fourth to scoop out the wax from my ears
with this platinum trowel.
I will pay them in yellow pears.

Where can I find seven small girls to be good dears,
where can I find them?
A fifth one to clip the nails of my toes
with these sharp silver shears,
a sixth to blow my enormous nose
with this satin sheet.
I will pay them in plums.

But the seventh girl will stand on the palm of my
     hand,
singing and dancing,
and I will love the tiny music of her voice,
her sweet little jigs.
I will pay her in grapes and kumquats and figs.
Where can I find her?
Where can I find seven small girls to be pets?

Carol Ann Duffy

Sardines

You slip behind your parents' clothes
    in nineteen sixty-eight,
pull shut the wardrobe door, then
    curl into a ball.
                    You wait.

It's very still in there. So quiet.
    Your chin rests on your knees.
A long fur-coat is tickling
    so much you want to sneeze.

A year goes by. Neil Armstrong walks
    the surface of the moon
as slow as honey, while you think
    'Someone will find me soon!'

You fiddle with your father's ties.
    The earth crawls round the sun
and footsteps pass the wardrobe door.
    – It could be anyone!

The world outside turns decimal
    and all the old coins go
the way of dinosaurs, of early
    morning mist, of snow.

It's very quiet in there. So still.
　　Your knees support your chin
while you whisper, 'Any minute now
　　someone will burst in . . .'

Fashions change: hemlines fall and rise.
　　Hands sometimes reach inside
to take a shirt or dress away –
　　the door is opened wide

and then it's closed, and then it's dark
　　once more. Leaves grow. Leaves fall.
The earth crawls round the sun again.
　　(You almost *hear* it crawl.)

One day in nineteen eighty-five
　　you think about your life
alone; but there's room for neither
　　children nor a wife

in there. It's very still. So quiet.
　　Your chin rests on your knees.
Sometimes you whistle in that dark
　　like wind through broken trees.

'No one's going to find,' you say,
　　'my perfect hiding-place.
Not now.' It's nineteen ninety-nine.
　　The planet spins through space,

the trees grow fat with overcoats
   and you, you droop until
(at last) you fall asleep.
                    Good night.
It's quiet in there, and still.
So still.
            So very still.

Stephen Knight

Secret Poem

My secret is made of –
the fingertips of clouds,
the silence between heartbeats
found at a hospital bedside,
the hangman's gloves,
the stoat's bright eye,
the bullet as it slices
through the winter wind.

I found it –
on the edge of a lemon's bite,
clutched in the centre of a crocus,
held in a crisp packet,
crumpled at the side of the road
where the nettles stab
their sharp barbs
at the innocent child's hand.

This secret can –
prise open hearts made of steel,
smooth a stormy sea flat,
capture the wind,
cup the moon's shine
in an empty palm,
break apart Mount Everest
till it is powder
in a lover's pocket.

If I lost
this secret –
even the lonely mountain goat
would bleat . . .

Pie Corbett

All Creatures

I just can't seem to help it,
I love creatures – great and small,
But it's ones that others do not like
I love the best of all.
I like creepy crawly beetles
And shiny black-backed bugs,
Gnats and bats and spiders,
And slimy fat black slugs.
I like chirpy little crickets
And buzzing bumblebees,
Lice and mice and ladybirds,
And tiny jumping fleas.
I like wasps and ants and locusts,
Centipedes and snails,
Moles and voles and earwigs
And rats with long pink tails.

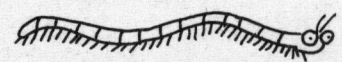

I like giant moths with dusty wings
And maggots fat and white,
Worms and germs and weevils,
And fireflies in the night.
No, I just can't seem to help it,
To me not one's a pest,
It's ones that others do not like,
I seem to love the best.

So it makes it rather difficult,
It's enough to make me cry,
Because my job's in pest control,
And I just couldn't hurt a fly.

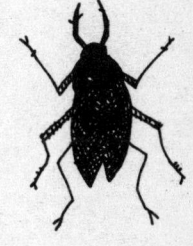

Gervase Phinn

Glove on a Spiked Railing

Rescued, out in the cold,
five knitted fingers'
frosty glitter
won't abandon hope
wherever now may be
the hand that fits them
wearing unfamiliar numbness
like a second skin.

They seem to say
exactly what I feel
without you,
stuck here, waving
to my other half,
not given up just yet
but frozen stiff.

John Mole

Thaw

The white garden
softens to green again
and cries silently.

Fred Sedgwick

Castle to be Built in the Woods

1. Choose a wood.

2. Make a clearing
   near a stream.

3. Dig a moat.
   Make it deep, wide.
   Fill it with water. One bridge only.

4. Lay solid foundations for your castle.
   Then build strong buttresses, stout keeps
   and tall towers with crenellations
   around the high battlements.

5. Make sure your castle has servants such as
   clerks, tailors, nurses, messengers,
   bootmakers, brewers, and a barber.
   You will need to lay down stores
   of food, wine, wax, spices and herbs.

6. An airy church inside the castle grounds
   and a dark dungeon deep below ground
   will mean that you can have
   Heaven and Hell at your fingertips.
   Don't forget to stock your arsenal with
   swords, daggers, lances, shields, battle-axes, etc.

7. Fire arrows at anyone who tries to
   attack your castle. Build murder-holes
   so that you can drop missiles and stones
   on the heads of your enemies.
   If you catch spies, lock them in
   the smallest, narrowest, smelliest room.
   Act ruthlessly. Behead people, frequently.

8. Hide treasure in a very secret part of the castle.
   Lock a beautiful princess in the tower.
   Force your fiercest dragon to guard both of these.
   Nominate a knight who will fight your battles
   so that you can never be injured or endangered.
   Employ a storyteller to make up tall tales
   and ghost stories about your castle.
   Marry someone and he can be the king.

John Rice

Summery

I love these pure white summer clouds
That drift across blue skies,
The knock-out scent of meadowsweet,
Willows full of sighs
When a breeze goes tickling branches,
And a lark decides to rise.

I love lying in long grasses
Which insects scuffle among,
Where bees helicopter over flowers,
And a stream glug-glugs along,
The lark above right out of sight
But cramming the sky with song.

This is the time for picnics,
Cherry-cake and tea
Poured hot from stubby vacuum flasks,
Plates balanced on your knee,
With cheese and brown-sauce sandwiches,
In the shade of a sycamore tree.

Matt Simpson

What Am I?

Sometimes I rhyme,
Sometimes I don't,
Sometimes I'll tease you,
Sometimes I won't,

Some-
times
I'm
Skin-
ny,

Sometimes I take

The form

Of a square,

Or   the   shape   of   a   sn-   ake

Sometimes I ramble,
Sometimes I rap,
Sometimes I force you
To join in and clap.

Sometimes I tell you
A tale sad and long,

Sometimes I sound
Like a comical song.

Sometimes I'm shouted,
Or silently read,
Sometimes I'll drift
Like a dream, through your head.

Sometimes I'm famous,
Sometimes I'm new,
But ALWAYS I'm written
For someone like YOU.

Clare Bevan

Answer?
I'm a POEM, of course!

If I Were the Leader

If I were the duke
Of oh-what-a-fluke
Then life would be a ball.

If I were the head
Of lying-in-bed
I'd never get up at all.

If I were in charge
Of everyone large
I wouldn't be pushed about.

If I were the boss
Of ever-so-cross
I'd stamp and scream and shout.

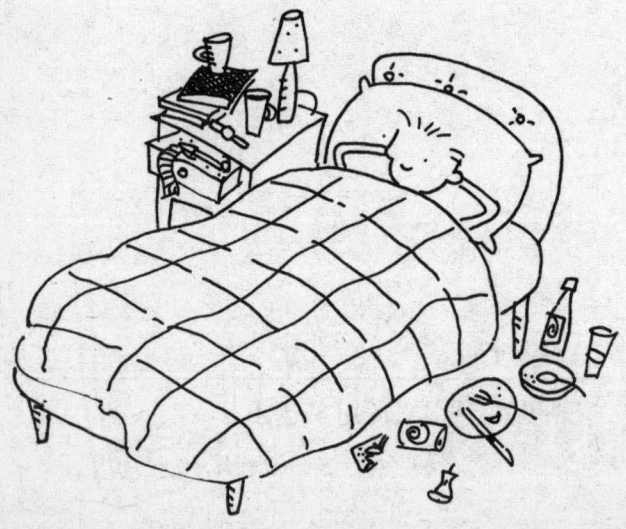

If I were the prince
Of only-a-rinse
There'd be no showers or baths.

If I were the lord
Of never-be-bored
We'd have no rain or maths.

If I were the chief
Of bacon-and-beef
I'd eat whatever I chose.

If I were the king
Of everything
I'd really get up your nose.

Nick Toczek

The World of Trees

(inspired by The Forest of Burnley)

Sycamore. Mountain Ash. Beech. Birch. Oak.

In the middle of the forest the trees stood.
And the beech knew the birch was there.
And the mountain ash breathed the same air
As the sycamore, and everywhere

The wind blew, the trees understood each other:
How the river made the old oak lean to the east,
How the felled beech changed the currents of the
   wind,
How the two common ash formed a canapé,

And grew in a complimentary way.
Between them they shared a full head of hair.
Some amber curls of the one could easily
belong to the other: twin trees, so similar.

Sycamore. Mountain Ash. Beech. Birch. Oak.

Some trees crouched in the forest waiting,
For another tree to die so that they could
Shoot up suddenly in that new space;
Stretch out comfortably for the blue sky.

Some trees grew mysterious mushroom fungi,
shoelace, honey, intricate as a grandmother's lace.
The wind fluttered the leaves; the leaves flapped their
    wings.
Birds flew from the trees. Sometimes they'd sing.

The tall trees, compassionate, understood everything:
Grief – they stood stock still, branches, drooped in
    despair.
Fear – they exposed their many roots, tugged their
    gold hair.
Anger – they shook in the storm, pointed their bony
    fingers.

Sycamore. Mountain Ash. Beech. Birch. Oak.

The trees knew each other's secrets.
In the deep green heart of the forest.
Each tree loved another tree best.
Each tree, happy to rest, leans a little to the east,

or to the west, when the moon loomed high above,
the big white eye of the woods.
And they stood together as one in the dark,
With the stars sparkling from their branches,

completely at ease, breathing in the cold night air
Swishing a little in the breeze,
Dreaming of glossy spring leaves
in the fine, distinguished company of trees.

Sycamore. Mountain Ash. Beech. Birch. Oak.

Jackie Kay

Football Dreaming

I'm
a striker racing,
a fullback chasing,
a winger crossing,
a captain bossing,
a wingback tackling,
a stopper shackling,
a halfback strolling,
a coach controlling,
a forward flicking,
a goalie kicking,
a linkman scheming,
a mad-fan dreaming
   on the
      morning bus
         to school.

Wes Magee

Jemima

Running down the garden path
Jemima, seven years old
Lifts her eyes to watch the sun
Drown in clouds of gold.
Sees her old friend smiling down
Through the chestnut tree
Her face among the branches smiles
White as ivory.
Jemima tells her secrets
Her breath is like a sigh
Wishing on a star that falls
Dying through the sky.
Jemima up the evening path
Through twilight bright as noon
Tells anyone who'll listen,
'I've been talking to the moon.'

Gareth Owen

Lock the Dairy Door!

Old Fox comes trotting over the hill
     Down from Caistor Tor,
On through the woods by the water-mill.
     Lock the dairy door!

He's an orange flame in the early light
     As he sneaks between the trees,
With his tail down low and his sharp eyes bright
     He sniffs the morning breeze.

Near to the farm he drops his speed.
     Head to the ground he goes.
There are hungry cubs in the den to feed.
     He twitches his clever nose.

The proud cock struts by the chicken run,
  Raises his head to the sky,
And lifts his voice to the morning sun,
  With, 'Fly sisters, fly!'

'Fly, sisters. Fly!
  To the perch in the old grain store.
A hungry fox is passing by.
  Lock the dairy door!'

Old Fox goes trotting past the farm
  Turns north, toward his lair.
Now no chicken will come to harm
  But rabbits – beware!

Gerard Benson

Cold Spell

for Ruth Underhill

'A cold spell,' said the weatherman
and my boiler's on the blink –
no central heating! I've just seen
a walrus in my kitchen sink.

P-p-p-p-penguins (not the chocolate kind)
are waddling down the hall,

whilst polar bears play on the stairs,
throwing giant snowballs.

A reindeer, with bright red nose,
is snoozing in the loo,
together with some Friesian cows
or are they eskimoos?

Two dozen elves fill up my shelves –
they're making too much noise –
wrapping up, then stacking up
gifts for girls and boys.

Yes, Father Christmas has moved
in to 36, The Crescent:
so be good children, my new job
is labelling the presents.

Mike Johnson

Giant's Eye View

(From the Grossmunster Tower, Zurich)

It's great to get a giant's eye view
of this city,
people down below not knowing
they're watched . . .

I'd like to reach down
and rearrange the streets.
Like a mischievous giant with elastic arms
I could de-rail trams, cause traffic jams,
move parked cars to different spaces,
wipe the smile from people's faces
by flipping them into the river
with my finger flicks . . .

With my giant's eye I could spy into skylights,
I could snoop in hidden courtyards.
I could block chimneys with my thumbs,
re-route smoke through the rooms below.

And all the birds thinking they're safe,
that the skyways belong to them . . .
Be gone gulls, scram pigeons,
there'll be no skywalking on my rooftops.

For one trifling moment
I'd be the hidden king of this city,
leave my giant's mark and feel the power
of the writer who scratched at the tower top:
ich war hier . . .
I WAS HERE!

Brian Moses

The Big Shed

A ramshackle den of clutter,
A mazy mixture of the useful and the useless,
The rubbish, the rusty, the wood and the mud.

At least three small sheds' worth
Of tongue and groove and four by two,
Dismantled the flat packed . . . well, sort of . . .
All jumbled zig-zag seesaw heaps.

The monster orange rotavator,
Its giant teeth caked with mud
Silent and untamed
I was never allowed to grapple this beast
Until I was at secondary school.

The dead red and white motor scooter
Complete with windshield and crash helmet
That Dad could never get to work
But Cousin Paul took and resurrected.

Stacks and stacks and stacks
Of multi-purpose bamboo canes
That would become arrows, guns or swords
Depending on last night's television.

Hay bales, musty, dusty and precarious
Transformed into forts, mountains or sheer rock faces
Depending on last night's television.

The bowed wooden barrel we broke
One summer holiday afternoon
When trying to walk inside it, the barrel over our
    heads
Because we were re-enacting an adventure from
    'Scooby Doo'.

The legend of 'Hairy Face'
Created then extended
From nothing to belief
Thanks to invented sightings and pretend happenings
All scratchings, creakings and whistlings became his.
No one really believed
Until they were left alone at dusk
When darkness extended its bony fingers,
Squeezing out remaining light
And 'Hairy Face' lurked in every single shadow.

Hide-and-seek became a game
With endless possibilities.
No two games identical our options knew few limits
As plastic sheets, piles of planks,
Pallets and potato sacks
Chimney pots and high hay stacks
Were rearranged so that youthful bodies were
    concealed that little bit longer.

We could lose ourselves for hours
In this ramshackle den of clutter,
That mazy mixture of the rubbish and the rusty
The wood, the mud, the useful, the useless
And us.

Paul Cookson

At Three in the Morning

When the fairground is silent and empty
And the candyfloss crowds have gone home,
The roundabout horses start dreaming
Of sun-swept sierras to roam,
Of canyons that clatter with hoof-beats,
Of rivers that shatter like glass,
Of galloping, never in circles again,
But straight through the heavens of grass.

Richard Edwards

Cornered

They chased me to the corner of the playground,
Where the air is colder
Because spiteful gusts of wind rush at the chain-link
    fence,
And dust blows in your face, rubs like sandpaper.

One tear escaped – then all was lost.
In for the kill, their teeth flashed through parted lips,
Their eyes narrowed in contempt.
I stared at the tarmac, cornered.

Rhymed insults sang a sneering song around my
    head
And, 'Baby! Baby! Baby!' boxed my ears
Until I was on the ground
My fingers spread over my face like prison bars.

Coral Rumble

Notes in Class

'You are like a red, red rose,'
he told her in his note.

'You are like a slimy slug,'
were the cruel words she wrote.

'My heart is yours for ever,'
he penned, 'forever true.'

'I would rather wash the dishes,'
she replied, 'than be with you.'

'You smell of summer flowers,'
he wrote, 'full blown and sweet.'

She wrote, 'You pong of sweaty socks
and even sweatier feet.'

He scrawled, 'My heart has broken
into pieces. I may die!'

She replied, 'Well why tell me,
I won't pretend I'd cry.'

He typed, 'My love has turned to hate.
My heart is now of stone.'

She scribbled, 'That's just typical.
I might have known you'd moan.'

Marian Swinger

The Tale of the Dog

'Man's Best Friend' –
That's what they call me;
And that's what I BELIEVED –
Until THE CAT arrived!

Whereas I have to be
'Faithful and obedient'
(SIT when ordered,
Fetch ANY ball or stick,

GROWL at unwelcome callers,
NEVER stay out at night)
For a few MISERABLE chocolate drops . . .

The CAT (on the other hand)
Can 'lounge around',
Preen herself FOR HOURS, Slink away disdainfully
Whenever visitors arrive,
And SCRATCH to pieces
ANYONE who strokes her
When she wants to go to sleep.
She STAYS AWAY

For **NIGHTS ON END** –
And always gets
A WARM WELCOME
When she returns!
It's none of the
'SIT!' 'STAY!' 'BAD DOG!'
Kind of talk
They keep dishing out to **ME** –
And she STILL gets fed
AND sheltered!

'Man's Best Friend', eh?
It looks like I
Shall have to do some
SERIOUS RE-THINKING
About THAT!

Trevor Harvey